P9-AOS-170

Charles M. Schulz

I've Been Traded for a Pizza?

HarperHorizon
An Imprint of HarperCollins*Publishers*

FARMINGDALE PUBLIC LIBRARY
116 MERRITTS ROAD
FARMINGDALE, N.Y. 11735

First published in 1998 by HarperCollins*Publishers* Inc. http://www.harpercollins.com

Copyright © 1998 United Feature Syndicate, Inc. All rights reserved.
HarperCollins ® and ♣ ® are trademarks of HarperCollins*Publishers* Inc. PEANUTS is a registered trademark of United Feature Syndicate, Inc.
PEANUTS © United Feature Syndicate, Inc. Based on the PEANUTS ® comic strip by Charles M. Schulz

http://www.unitedmedia.com
ISBN 0-694-00974-1
Printed in Canada.

"Okay, team, this is our first game. Let's hear some chatter out there. Let's show Peppermint Patty's team what kind of spirit we have!"

"Sorry I missed that one, Manager. I was hoping I'd catch it. Hope got in my eyes!"

"Okay, team, this should be an easy win—we're playing Chuck's team!"

"Sir, why do I always have to play right field?"

"It's traditional. The worst player always plays right field, and you're our worst player . . ."

". . . but you wear your glove well, Marcie."

"Thank you, Sir. I appreciate the compliment."

"Hey, Chuck, I'm calling to see if you're interested in trading right fielders."

"I hate baseball."

"Sure, I'll trade you Marcie for Lucy. Yeah, I know Marcie isn't very good . . ."

"I hate baseball."

". . . but she has a lot of enthusiasm . . ."

"Oh, how I hate baseball!"

"You what? You traded me for that stupid girl with the glasses?"

"You were robbed!"

"No, I think I got the better deal . . .
they agreed to throw in a pizza!"

"Hi, Charles, I'm your new right fielder. I've heard that you have sort of a weird team."

"Actually, Charles, I hate baseball. I'm only playing on your team because I've always been fond of you."

"Marcie, you should be out in right field."

"I'm happier standing here with you, Charles."

"But what if someone hits a ball to right field?"

"Who cares? I'm happy just standing here next to you, Charles."

"We don't win any games, but I have happy players."

"Hi there, Lucille. Welcome to my team! Why don't you get out there in right field, and I'll hit you a few flies."

"Do you take excuses?"

"Okay, Lucille, this next hitter is pretty good so keep your eye on the ball."

"That's hard to do when you keep moving it around."

"Get back out there in right field where you belong!"

"Women managers are even crabbier than men managers."

"Sorry I missed that one, Manager. Maybe my glove isn't big enough."

"Big enough? Ha! You know what you need?"

"I made a mistake, Chuck . . . I admit it. Lucy is the worst player I've ever seen! I know you traded her to me for Marcie and a pizza, but now I want to call the deal off. What do you say, Chuck?"

"I already ate the pizza."

"I hear I got traded back, Charles, so I just wanted to say goodbye. I guess I wasn't much help to your baseball team. I didn't score a single goal."